This book
belongs to

. . . . . . . . . . . . . . . . .

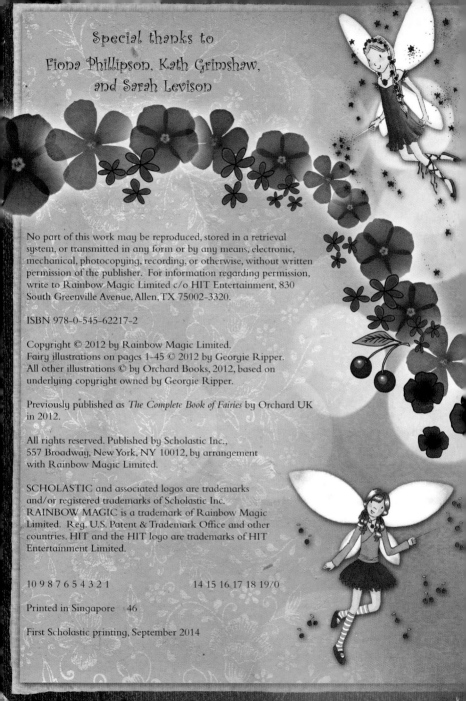

Special thanks to
Fiona Phillipson, Kath Grimshaw,
and Sarah Levison

ISBN 978-0-545-62217-2

10 9 8 7 6 5 4 3 2 1          14 15 16 17 18 19/0

Printed in Singapore    46

First Scholastic printing, September 2014

# The Ultimate Fairy Guide

SCHOLASTIC INC.

# Contents

Dear Reader,

I was the first fairy that Rachel and Kirsty found, and I am so glad they did! The girls have helped all the Rainbow Magic fairies so much, and we look upon them as our very special friends.

We fairies do not show ourselves easily to humans, and when we do it is only ever to children. It was a lucky chance Rachel and Kirsty met me during their vacation on Rainspell Island.

Always keep a lookout for fairies wherever you are. Peek inside flowers, look into the corners of frosty windows, check in the bottom of your closet and even in the folds of the curtains in your bedroom. You never know when we may need your help!

I hope we will meet you one day.

Lots of love,
Ruby XOXO

# Ruby
## the Red Fairy

The Rainbow Fairies help keep all colors beautiful and bright.

**Ruby's dress is made from hundreds of tiny rose petals!**

**Ruby's favorite foods are super-sweet strawberries and jam tarts.**

Ruby is very special to Rachel and Kirsty. She's the very first fairy they ever met! Ruby and her six rainbow sisters were banished from Fairyland by Jack Frost's spell. Rachel and Kirsty found Ruby by following a beautiful rainbow across Rainspell Island.

# Amber
## the Orange Fairy

When Amber uses her wand, it releases shimmering bubbles that smell like oranges!

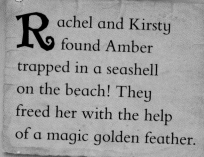

Rachel and Kirsty found Amber trapped in a seashell on the beach! They freed her with the help of a magic golden feather.

# Sunny
## the Yellow Fairy

Yellow butterflies emerge from Sunny's wand each time she waves it.

Jack Frost's spell sent Sunny tumbling into a beehive! Luckily, this friendly fairy had a great time with the bees and even made a very special bee friend named Queenie.

# Fern
## the Green Fairy

Fern's adventure took place in a secret garden! Rachel and Kirsty had to make their way through a maze to find Fern. With the help of some friendly animals and a magic fairy firework, Fern was finally reunited with her rainbow sisters!

**Fern's best friend is a gray squirrel named Fluffy!**

# Sky
## the Blue Fairy

**R**achel and Kirsty had to scare off some ice-skating goblins to rescue Sky from a frozen tide pool. Sky was so cold her rainbow sisters needed to form a fairy ring to bring back her magic sparkles.

Whenever Sky waves her wand, a shower of sparkling blue stars appears.

When fairies form a fairy ring their magic joins together and becomes very powerful!

Inky's magic turns everything she touches a beautiful indigo color!

# Inky
## the Indigo Fairy

**I**nky's adventure took place in the enchanted Land of Sweets! In this story the girls and Izzy met the Sugarplum Fairy and rode in a pink bubblegum balloon.

# Heather
## the Violet Fairy

Rachel and Kirsty had to reunite Heather with her rainbow sisters before their vacation on Rainspell Island came to an end! Luckily, a magic ride on a merry-go-round led them to the little fairy. But then the fairies had to face Jack Frost and his gang of goblins!

Heather's magic allows her to create fizzing violet bubbles. These can grow large enough to trap Jack Frost!

# Crystal
## the Snow Fairy

When Jack Frost and his goblins took the Weather Fairies' feathers, the weather in Fairyland and the human world turned totally topsy-turvy! Rachel and Kirsty had to help Crystal find her magic snow feather and return it to Doodle the weather-vane rooster.

At the start of Crystal's story, Queen Titania gives Rachel and Kirsty two lockets filled with magic fairy dust.

The girls use this fairy dust in lots of their Rainbow Magic adventures!

# Abigail
## the Breeze Fairy

**I**n the hands of a troublesome goblin, Abigail's breeze feather caused chaos at the Wetherbury Summer Festival. With the help of a puppy named Twiglet, the girls and Abigail found the magic feather high in the sky!

Breezy autumn is Abigail's favorite time of year — she loves to fly among the falling golden leaves!

# Pearl
## the Cloud Fairy

**T**he magic of the cloud feather made everyone very grumpy when it was taken from its rightful fairy owner, Pearl!

Pearl's favorite color is pale pink, the color of sunsets.

# Goldie
## the Sunshine Fairy

Goldie really is a little ray of sunshine! She's super-smiley, warmhearted, and full of giggles.

Everyone loves sunshine! But when Goldie's magic sunshine feather was stolen from Doodle, the sun shone so much that it was way too hot in Wetherbury.

# Evie
## the Mist Fairy

**E**vie's mist feather creates sparkly wisps of mist that make things look very pretty! But in the hands of goblins, the feather caused all kinds of misty mischief.

Fairy children love to play hide-and-seek in Evie's mist!

Goblins are scared of mist because they think pogwurzels will sneak up behind them!

# Storm
## the Lightning Fairy

**R**achel and Kirsty had a very dramatic adventure with Storm the Lightning Fairy! They came face-to-face with a mean goblin inside a dusty, old museum.

# Hayley
## the Rain Fairy

After Jack Frost took Hayley's magic rain feather, the rain just wouldn't stop falling! With Hayley's help, the girls paddled through a flood to return all seven magic weather feathers to Doodle.

**Hayley's favorite movie is *Singin' in the Rain*!**

# Cherry
## the Cake Fairy

The Party Fairies love to entertain!

Queen Titania and King Oberon's 1,000th anniversary as rulers of Fairyland was a very happy occasion. The Party Fairies were on hand to make the celebrations extra special! But Jack Frost was determined to spoil the fun. Rachel and Kirsty had to help Cherry find her missing party bag so she could bake a magic cake fit for the royal couple!

Cherry loves all desserts but her very favorite is Black Forest cake. Yummy!

# Melodie
## the Music Fairy

Goblins love music. But they're tone-deaf and have no sense of rhythm!

**P**oor Kirsty's ballet recital was almost ruined when a goblin stole Melodie's party bag and caused musical mayhem!

With a wave of Melodie's wand, instruments start to play all by themselves!

# Grace
## the Glitter Fairy

**W**hen Grace's magic bag went missing, all glittery party decorations lost their sparkle.

Grace's favorite party foods are Cherry's cupcakes — they're covered in edible glitter!

# Honey
## the Candy Fairy

N o party is complete without some delicious sweet treats. Honey's adventure took place in Mrs. Twist's Candy Shop, which is full of all the candy you could ever dream of! But when a goblin tried to snatch Honey's party bag, the store was in a very sticky situation.

Honey loves inventing new candy. She has lots of fun taste-testing her creations with the other Party Fairies!

# Polly
## the Party Fun Fairy

Polly the Party Fun Fairy makes sure that every party has lots of games for everyone to enjoy! So it was very important for the girls to help Polly find her party bag when it went missing.

When Polly uses the fairy dust in her party bag, beautiful balloons appear!

Polly's very favorite party game is Hot Potato.

# Phoebe
## the Fashion Fairy

Phoebe makes sure that everyone looks fairy fabulous at parties and celebrations with fashionable dresses and amazing accessories!

The silk used to make Phoebe's dress is from magic silkworms. The dress glimmers and shimmers in the light!

# Jasmine
## the Present Fairy

J asmine's magic makes presents and prizes perfect for everyone! This special magic power has to be looked after very carefully. Rachel and Kirsty had to protect her bag and get to the king and queen's anniversary party on time.

Jasmine is named after a delicate, beautifully scented flower.

At the end of Jasmine's book, Rachel and Kirsty are each given a musical jewelry box by the fairy king and queen.

# India
## the Moonstone Fairy

The Jewel Fairies use their gems to help their friends in Fairyland.

The Jewel Fairies each have a precious stone. India's beautiful moonstone helps make sure that everyone has sweet dreams. When Jack Frost stole the seven magic jewels, Rachel and Kirsty had to help the Jewel Fairies return them to Queen Titania's tiara — or all fairy magic would have faded away!

When all of the Jewel Fairies' jewels are in Queen Titania's tiara, a magic rainbow is formed once a year. The fairies use this to recharge their magic!

# Scarlett
## the Garnet Fairy

Scarlett's jewel has the power to make things bigger and smaller. If her garnet wasn't returned to the tiara, Kirsty and Rachel might have stayed fairy-sized forever!

Scarlett and Ruby once hosted a party where everyone had to dress in red!

# Emily
## the Emerald Fairy

Emily's adventure took place in a wonderful toy shop! But with the missing jewel affecting Emily's special ability to see into the future, things were not always what they seemed . . .

# Chloe
## the Topaz Fairy

**C**hloe's golden topaz disappeared on Halloween. With Chloe's magic jewel missing, her ability to change one thing into another caused all kinds of tricks and treats at a costume shop in Tippington.

Chloe's jewel is a beautiful golden color, but topaz can actually come in many different colors!

# Amy
## the Amethyst Fairy

**A**my's magic amethyst controls appearing and disappearing — she can make things invisible! When Amy's jewel went missing, the girls had a very odd adventure, high up in a tree house!

Amy sometimes uses her magic to help Polly the Party Fun Fairy with her games!

# Sophie
## the Sapphire Fairy

**S**ophie's sparkling sapphire controls wishing magic! With her jewel lost somewhere in the human world, wishes everywhere were in a terrible mess.

Sophie is best friends with Zara the Starlight Fairy. The sapphires that flow from Sophie's wand look so beautiful in Zara's starlight!

# Lucy
## the Diamond Fairy

I n the final Jewel Fairies' adventure, Rachel and Kirsty traveled to Fairyland to help Lucy find her diamond, which controls flying magic. The girls had to avoid scary Jack Frost's ice bolts so they could return the diamond to Queen Titania's tiara!

The girls love flying but Kirsty sometimes finds it scary, especially when she's a fairy and Jack Frost is chasing her!

# Katie
## the Kitten
## Fairy

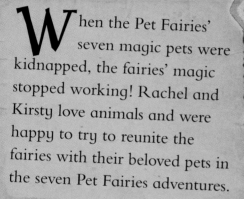

When the Pet Fairies' seven magic pets were kidnapped, the fairies' magic stopped working! Rachel and Kirsty love animals and were happy to try to reunite the fairies with their beloved pets in the seven Pet Fairies adventures.

Kirsty has a kitten named Pearl.

There are three fairies who have cute pet cats!

The Pet Fairies make sure that all pets in Fairyland and the human world have happy homes.

# Bella
## the Bunny Fairy

If a bunny is ever in trouble, it's Bella to the rescue! Her enchanted helper is a fluffy rabbit named Misty, who twitches her nose and is always changing color.

**Misty lives in a cozy burrow underneath Bella's pretty toadstool house.**

# Georgia
## the Guinea Pig Fairy

Georgia's adventure took place on Strawberry Farm. Rachel and Kirsty had to deal with some very odd sheep to reunite Georgia and her supercute guinea pig, Sparky!

**Guinea pigs are very sociable animals. Sparky loves to play with all the other magic pets!**

# Lauren
## the Puppy Fairy

Rachel has a dog named Buttons!

The girls were having a wonderful time at the Wetherbury Spring Fair when they met Sunny, Lauren's magic puppy. But it was a race against time to reunite him with Lauren before the goblins could snatch him!

In Fairyland, pets choose their owners — unlike in the human world, where it's the other way around!

# Harriet
## the Hamster Fairy

Three goblins set a tricky trap for Twinkle, the magic hamster, in Harriet's adventure. Kirsty and Rachel had to reach him before the goblins could!

# Molly
## the Goldfish Fairy

There were some very sneaky goblins disguised as gnomes in Molly's story. They took Flash, Molly's magic goldfish! Luckily, Flash was very smart and managed to swim back to Molly.

# Penny
## the Pony Fairy

Rachel and Kirsty were having a nice pony ride in the forest when Glitter, the magic pony, arrived in a cloud of fairy magic! Unfortunately a group of seven goblins threatened to spook all the ponies with their mischievous ways.

Both Rachel and Kirsty love horse riding. They have lots of horsey fun with Helena the Horse-riding Fairy!

# Megan
## the Monday Fairy

The Fun Day Fairies' magic keeps the calendar from falling into chaos.

**W**hen the girls met Megan, Jack Frost had taken the Fun Day Fairies' seven magic flags. Without them, the Fun Day Fairies couldn't make any day *anywhere* enjoyable. They had to find their flags and charge their wands — or lose their powers forever!

Every morning, Francis the Royal Time Guard looks in the Fairyland Book of Days to check which day it is.

# Tara
## the Tuesday Fairy

With Tara's magic flag missing, this fairy couldn't help anyone have a good time on Tuesdays! That meant that Rachel's field day was no fun at all.

Tara is Tia the Tulip Fairy's best friend. These two fairies love to fly around Fairyland together!

# Willow
## the Wednesday Fairy

I n this adventure, Rachel and Kirsty had to find Willow's flag at the Tippington Arts and Crafts Fair. Unfortunately, it was the perfect place for goblins to hide!

Willow's flag is one of the prettiest of them all. It's green and gold, and covered in glitter.

# Thea
## the Thursday Fairy

Thea's favorite thing to do on Thursday mornings is to teach young fairies how to dance a fairy jig!

Thea's story takes place in an aquarium! It was a magical place for the girls to visit — there were seahorses, crabs, sharks, otters, and a reef to see . . . and some troublesome goblins! They wanted Thea's Fun Day flag so they could ruin Thursdays for everyone.

Kirsty and Rachel love to swim through the water with their fairy friends. Fairy magic makes them warm and dry as soon as they're back on land.

# Felicity
## the Friday Fairy

Felicity is very artistic and teaches the other Fun Day Fairies how to paint and draw.

**E**veryone loves Fridays — but when Felicity's beautiful lilac flag went missing, no one in either the fairy or human worlds had that fun Friday feeling!

# Sienna
## the Saturday Fairy

All of the Fun Day Fairies' flags have a picture of the sun on them. Everyone feels full of sunshine and happiness when the flags work their magic!

**E**ven a fashion show couldn't make the Saturday in Sienna's story fun! Luckily, her flag was somewhere backstage at the show — but so was a gang of goblins . . .

# Sarah
## the Sunday Fairy

In this final Fun Day adventure, a picnic at Windy Lake was the girls' last chance to reunite Sarah with her magic flag. But first they had to persuade a certain frosty visitor to help them!

At the end of the Fun Day adventures, Queen Titania gave Rachel and Kirsty each a glittering kite! Every time they fly their kites, the girls think of their fairy friends.

Phoebe the Fashion Fairy uses her magic to change the colors of Sarah's striped tights for special occasions!

# Tia
## the Tulip Fairy

The Petal Fairies make sure that flowers everywhere grow beautifully!

When Jack Frost stole the Petal Fairies' magic petals and scattered them around the human world, Rachel and Kirsty had a tough job ahead of them. First, they had to return Tia's tulip petal to her — and fast!

Jack Frost secretly wishes he had a green thumb. He wants pretty flowers to grow in his icy garden!

# Pippa
## the Poppy Fairy

**P**ippa's adventure took place in a pretty flower shop, but with the magic petals missing, all the flowers were droopy! The girls had to outwit a whole gang of goblins to find Pippa's poppy petal and return it to Fairyland.

# Louise
## the Lily Fairy

**I**n this book, Rachel and Kirsty row a boat on a lake full of lily pads. But with Louise's magic petal in the hands of the pesky goblins, the lily pads had no beautiful flowers.

# Charlotte
## the Sunflower Fairy

**C**harlotte's cheery sunflower is a fairy favorite. When Jack Frost took her magic petal, everyone was very unhappy to see her stunning flowers wilting. It was very important for Rachel and Kirsty to help Charlotte get her petal back so her flowers could stand tall again!

Even though Charlotte takes care of yellow sunflowers, her favorite color is blue!

# Olivia
## the Orchid Fairy

The orchid is a very delicate flower. When Rachel and Kirsty met Olivia, they had to help her get her blue-and-purple petal back from the goblins before the clumsy creatures destroyed it.

Each magic petal protects a certain type of flower, but all the petals take care of every other flower and plant in the world, too!

# Danielle
## the Daisy Fairy

In her adventure, Danielle and the girls had to dodge a storm of icy hailstones to get her magic petal back from the goblins! Luckily, the fairy friends had some help from a very long, magic daisy chain!

# Ella
## the Rose Fairy

A flower show set in some beautiful gardens was where Kirsty and Rachel had their adventure with Ella the Rose Fairy. In this final Petal Fairies book, the girls had to flutter through the Chaney Court Hedge Maze — and come face-to-face with chaos-causing goblins — to find Ella's beautiful petal.

For the other Petal Fairies' birthdays, Ella sews fallen rose petals together to make pretty gifts.

# Bethany
## the Ballet Fairy

The Dance Fairies all love to sway and move!

Bethany teaches the young fairies how to dance. They look so cute practicing their pliés in tiny fairy tutus!

In this book, Kirsty and Rachel are going to see *Swan Lake*, a very famous ballet about a swan princess.

All seven Dance Fairies were cast into the human world by Jack Frost. *And* he took their magic ribbons! Nobody could enjoy dancing in the human world or in Fairyland until Rachel and Kirsty helped the fairies get all of their ribbons back.

# Jade
## the Disco Fairy

**J**ade is a real disco star in her swirly green bell-bottoms and funky top! In her book, Kirsty's school was hosting a dance. Even though Jade always looks ready to hit the dance floor, when her magic ribbon went missing she wasn't in much of a party mood.

Jack Frost stole the Dance Fairies' ribbons because he wanted his goblins to dance well at his party!

# Rebecca
## the Rock 'n' Roll Fairy

**K**irsty's parents were going to a rock 'n' roll dance party in this adventure, but the girls knew that if Rebecca's ribbon wasn't returned to her quickly, the dance would be a disaster!

The Dance Fairies

37

# Tasha
## the Tap Dance Fairy

**R**achel and Kirsty were at a Wetherbury College open house in this adventure when a group of toe-tapping goblins attracted their attention! The girls and Tasha had to think of a plan to distract the goblins so they could return the magic ribbon to its rightful owner.

Tasha loves to perform in front of her fairy friends. Sometimes she teams up with Vanessa the Choreography Fairy, and together they put on a show!

# Jessica
## the Jazz Fairy

Jessica's beautiful pink dress is a chic 1920s style. Her loose-fitting outfit means she can perform high kicks and splits.

The girls were invited to a grown-up party in this book, with a cool jazz band. But Rachel and Kirsty knew that because Jessica's magic ribbon was missing, disaster would soon strike!

# Serena
## the Salsa Fairy

Fun-loving Serena brings every celebration to life with her supercool Latin dance style! But with her dance ribbon missing, the girls were worried that the Wetherbury Fiesta would be an absolute disaster!

# Isabelle
## the Ice Dance Fairy

Isabelle and Poppy the Piano Fairy are best friends. Poppy creates magic tinkling songs for Isabelle to skate along to!

This icy adventure starred seven ice-skating goblins! They caused chaos at the Glacier Ice Rink and ruined the show for everyone. The final dance ribbon had to be returned to Isabelle before any more disasters took place.

# Helena
## the Horse-riding Fairy

The Sports Fairies keep all things athletic running smoothly.

Rachel and Kirsty were about to go horse riding when they were magically whisked to Fairyland and introduced to seven new fairy friends! The Sports Fairies were in trouble — Jack Frost's goblins had stolen the seven magic sports objects. With these missing, the Fairy Olympics couldn't begin, and no one could enjoy any of their favorite sports!

The Fairy Olympics are held in the Fairyland Arena, a magic place that changes to suit whatever sport is being played!

The winner of the Fairy Olympics is awarded a magnificent golden cup full of luck. Jack Frost really wanted to get his hands on it!

# Stacey
## the Soccer Fairy

In Stacey's book, the girls watched a Tippington Rovers soccer game with Rachel's mom and dad. But some goblins were also at the soccer field, and they had Stacey's magic soccer ball.

# Zoe
## the Skating Fairy

With Zoe's magic shoelace missing, all skaters and skateboarders were in trouble! In this exciting adventure, it was up to the girls to help find the lace. Then Zoe could make skating fun again!

# Brittany
## the Basketball Fairy

Basketball is normally a fun and popular team sport, but with Brittany's magic basketball missing, nobody was having a good time! While helping Brittany, Rachel and Kirsty met a team called The Mean Green Basketball Team. The girls were very suspicious! Green normally means goblins, and goblins mean trouble.

**Brittany loves playing pickup games with the other Sports Fairies.**

# Samantha
## the Swimming Fairy

**Normally, goblins don't like getting wet, but with Samantha's magic goggles close by, they have lots of fun swimming!**

Swimming is the perfect sport to enjoy on a summer day! But with Samantha's magic goggles missing, Kirsty and Rachel were on high alert when they went for a dip at Aqua World!

# Alice
## the Tennis Fairy

In Alice's exciting book, Tippington Tennis Club was taken over by troops of tennis-playing goblins! Rachel and Kirsty had the tricky task of helping Alice get her magic racket back.

**Alice has a mean backhand — and an even better serve!**

# Gemma
## the Gymnastics Fairy

**B**y the time Kirsty and Rachel met Gemma, it was almost time for the Fairy Olympics to start! Gemma's magic hoop was missing and needed to be returned to Fairyland — otherwise Jack Frost and his goblins could still win the games.

The Sports Fairies wanted to teach the goblins a very important lesson — you don't have to cheat to enjoy sports!

# Poppy
## the Piano Fairy

The Music Fairies protect music in both Fairyland and the human world.

Kirsty and Rachel love listening to music! So they were shocked to learn that music everywhere could be ruined because Jack Frost had stolen all of the magic musical instruments from the Royal School of Music. In Poppy's book, he formed a band with his goblins and was going to enter a music contest in the human world. The girls had to stop him!

# Ellie
## the Guitar Fairy

**E**llie loves playing funky songs on her electric guitar! But when it fell into the hands of the goblins, even she couldn't play a note without it sounding awful.

# Fiona
## the Flute Fairy

**F**iona the Flute Fairy fluttered magically out of a sparkly card at the start of her book! She knew her magic flute was nearby, but had to ask for help from Rachel and Kirsty so she could get it back before the goblins caused any more trouble.

**The enchanting music that comes from Fiona's flute makes people want to follow it!**

# Danni
## the Drum Fairy

Rachel and Kirsty were excited to star in a music video in this book! They knew they had to stay alert if they were going to find another missing magic musical instrument. Luckily, the goblins soon appeared with Danni's magic drumsticks.

The Music Fairies' instruments are still fairy-sized in the human world, so they can be very hard to spot!

Whenever Danni uses her wand, lots of tiny drumsticks appear!

# Maya
## the Harp Fairy

**M**aya's elegant harp plays magic musical melodies! But when the magic harp went missing, harp music everywhere sounded awful. Rachel and Kirsty had to help Maya find her instrument before their friend's wedding was ruined.

Maya's favorite color is yellow.

# Victoria
## the Violin Fairy

**T**he girls had a sneak peek at Frosty's Gobolicious Band in this fairy tale! With Victoria's magic violin nearby to keep them in harmony, the band sounded great. But the girls had to return the violin to Victoria so *all* music could be harmonious.

# Sadie
## the Saxophone Fairy

S adie's story was the final Music Fairies' adventure, and it was time for the National Talent Competition! With Sadie's saxophone still missing, the girls knew that Frosty's Gobolicious Band could easily win the competition, putting Fairyland in danger. Kirsty and Rachel had to work hard and save the day, without ruining the competition for everyone else!

Even when the talent competition is over, Jack Frost still thinks he is a super-talented musician!

# Ashley
## the Dragon Fairy

The Magical Animal Fairies need their animals back to keep the human world safe —and to keep Fairyland a secret!

Ashley's young dragon is named Sizzle. He protects the magic power of imagination.

Rachel and Kirsty met the Magical Animal Fairies while they were attending an outdoor adventure camp. They discovered that Jack Frost had stolen seven young magical animals. The baby animals were all being trained to use a particular type of magic so they could help everyone enjoy life. The animals escaped Jack Frost's icy clutches — but then got lost in the human world!

Ashley has a Chinese dragon on her pant leg. This type of dragon is said to ward off evil spirits!

When Sizzle sneezes, small flames appear. All of Fairyland must watch out when the baby dragon has a cold!

# Lara
## the Black Cat Fairy

**D**uring a camp activity, Rachel and Kirsty found Lara's magical animal. Lucky, an adorable little black cat, has the power to bring good luck. While she was missing, bad luck was happening everywhere!

# Erin
## the Phoenix Fairy

**I**n Erin's adventure, the girls spotted a very unusual bird by a stream. It was Giggles the phoenix, whose magic protects humor. Rachel, Kirsty, and Erin had to try to reach Giggles before the goblins found him.

# Rihanna
## the Seahorse Fairy

**R**ihanna's magic seahorse, Bubbles, helps protect friendship — which is very important to both fairies and humans! When Bubbles isn't in Fairyland with his fairy, friendships everywhere suffer. So when Jack Frost stole Bubbles, Rachel and Kirsty had to find the little seahorse and reunite him with Rihanna.

**Rihanna's magic allowed the girls to breathe underwater!**

**Seahorses usually live in the ocean, but because Bubbles is a magic seahorse he can swim in lakes and rivers, too!**

# Sophia
## the Snow Swan Fairy

The girls were on a night-time walk at camp when a shimmering swan caught their eyes! They had to cross a beautiful waterfall and reach Sophia's baby swan, Belle, before the goblins did.

Belle's magic spreads compassion.

# Leona
## the Unicorn Fairy

Leona's magic animal is Twisty, the baby unicorn — he looks like a white pony! Twisty's magic came in very handy when a careless goblin hurt Rachel's wrist.

Leona and Helena the Horse-riding Fairy spend hours braiding the manes of their horse friends!

# Caitlin
## the Ice Bear Fairy

Jack Frost stole the magical animals because he knew the world would be a miserable place without them.

It was a chilly final day at the adventure camp and the girls had a big hill to climb! From the top of the hill they were hoping to spot the final missing magic animal, Crystal, the ice bear cub. But Jack Frost was also nearby with his frosty magic, hoping to find the little bear first.

# Nicole
## the Beach Fairy

The Earth
Fairies keep
the world clean
and green!

In the Earth Fairies' adventures, Rachel and Kirsty asked the fairies for their help! They returned to Rainspell Island for a vacation and were very upset to see that the beautiful beach was covered in litter. They knew they needed some magic to help them clean up the environment and show others how to do the same. But the last thing Jack Frost wanted was more interfering fairies.

At the start of this adventure, the Earth Fairies are still in training!

# Isabella
## the Air Fairy

**I**t's Isabella's job to make sure that the air humans and fairies breathe is as clean as possible! In her adventure, Rachel and Kirsty help Isabella clean up the air around Seabury.

# Edie
## the Garden Fairy

**G**ardens are important places. They provide safe homes for lots of plants and wildlife. When Rachel and Kirsty met Edie, they all volunteered to create a special garden. But Jack Frost had other plans . . .

Edie's mom is head gardener for the royal fairy household!

# Coral
## the Reef Fairy

Coral's emerald ankle bracelets were a birthday gift from the Jewel Fairies.

Coral joined the girls for a wonderful underwater adventure in this book! The girls traveled magically to a warm, tropical ocean many hundreds of miles away from Rainspell Island. They had to help Coral teach an important lesson to some very destructive goblins.

# Lily
## the Rain Forest Fairy

The girls were on a nature walk when they were whisked to an exotic rain forest with the help of Lily's fairy magic. They met many amazing creatures!

# Milly
## the River Fairy

Milly and Hayley the Rain Fairy are the very best of friends. These water-loving fairies like to splash around in rivers and puddles!

Milly had to get her wand back from Jack Frost so she could make all rivers clean and healthy. But first she needed the girls to help her outwit the goblins!

# Carrie
## the Snow Cap Fairy

Carrie's adventure is the last in the Earth Fairies' series! Rachel and Kirsty had only one wand left to find but Jack Frost was determined to hang on to it. Carrie and the girls had to convince the Ice Lord to return the wand.

Carrie's jacket is fake fur — she loves animals too much to wear real fur!

Carrie and Crystal the Snow Fairy have friendly competitions to see who can create the biggest and sparkliest snowballs!

# Ally
## the Dolphin Fairy

The Ocean Fairies help protect oceans everywhere!

Each of the seven Ocean Fairies has an ocean animal as a companion. These animals lead each fairy to a piece of the golden conch shell!

The girls were at the start of a beach vacation when they received a magic invitation to the Fairyland Ocean Gala! They learned that Shannon the Ocean Fairy plays a magic tune on the golden conch shell each year to make everything harmonious in all the oceans. But Jack Frost's clumsy goblins had stolen the shell and broken it into pieces. The Ocean Fairies needed Rachel and Kirsty's help!

# Amelie
## the Seal Fairy

**A** magic, sparkly light in a lantern led Rachel and Kirsty to Amelie! This little fairy knew her seal, Silky, was nearby, which meant the shell piece was close by, too. But so were some goblins dressed as pirates!

# Pia
## the Penguin Fairy

**P**ia took the girls on a wintry trip to the South Pole! But the girls found that everything was topsy-turvy because the conch shell hadn't been played. All the animals were very confused and in the wrong place!

# Tess
## the Sea Turtle Fairy

**When Tess waves her wand, lots of tiny turtles appear!**

**A** tropical island is the setting for this fairy adventure! Tess knew that her ocean animal, a beautiful turtle named Pearl, was near the fourth piece of the missing conch shell. Rachel and Kirsty had to help get the shell piece back to Fairyland. But first they had to help hundreds of baby turtles and deal with three very scared goblins!

**The silly goblins think that baby turtles are small pogwurzels!**

# Stephanie
## the Starfish Fairy

In this book, it was time for the girls to enjoy some stargazing. But there was only one star the girls wanted to spot — Stephanie's magic starfish, Spike!

# Whitney
## the Whale Fairy

**Whitney and Fin patrol the seas, making sure every whale is safe and happy.**

Ahoy there! Rachel and Kirsty were on board an old-fashioned sailing ship when they helped Whitney. There was a lot to see, including a pod of killer whales! One of the whales looked strangely sparkly, so the girls knew that a missing piece of the magic shell was close by.

# Courtney
## the Clownfish Fairy

I t was almost time for Rachel and Kirsty's vacation to end when they met Courtney and her clownfish, Squirt. They visited a magic underwater fair, but Jack Frost and lots of goblins were also there searching for the golden conch shell!

**When Courtney appears in the story, she's inside a fish-shaped balloon!**

**At the end of their ocean adventures the girls are each given a beautiful conch shell as a gift from Queen Titania and King Oberon.**

# Ava
## the Sunset Fairy

The Night Fairies have a special job, protecting the time between dusk and dawn.

Jack Frost stole the Night Fairies' magic dust because he was scared of the dark and wanted daytime to last forever!

Kirsty and Rachel were visiting Camp Stargaze for a week with their families when they spotted a very strange green sunset . . . they just knew Jack Frost was to blame!

If it wasn't for Ava's sunbeam dust, there would be nighttime chaos everywhere!

# Lexi
## the Firefly Fairy

The girls went on a nighttime stroll to the Twinkling Tree in this book, but with Lexi's bag of magic twilight dust missing, the Twinkling Tree had lost its shine.

# Zara
## the Starlight Fairy

Rachel and Kirsty spotted a strange constellation in Camp Stargaze's observatory at the start of this story. With Zara's bag of stardust missing, the stars were all mixed up.

# Morgan
## the Midnight Fairy

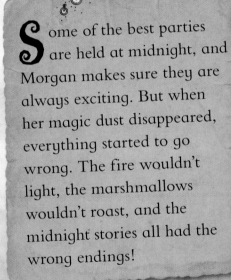

In this story, the goblins have an amazing feast with the help of Morgan's magic fairy dust.

Some of the best parties are held at midnight, and Morgan makes sure they are always exciting. But when her magic dust disappeared, everything started to go wrong. The fire wouldn't light, the marshmallows wouldn't roast, and the midnight stories all had the wrong endings!

Morgan's dress is the color of the sky at midnight!

# Nia
## the Night Owl Fairy

**A**ll kinds of animals are awake at nighttime, but with Nia's magic bag missing, the behavior of nighttime and daytime animals went haywire!

# Anna
## the Moonbeam Fairy

**M**oonlight is the most magical of lights, but in Anna's story the silly goblins tried to make their own moon! It was up to the girls to stop them and return Anna's moon dust to her.

**Without Anna's moon dust, even the fairies sleep all day!**

# Sabrina
## the Sweet Dreams Fairy

Sabrina has such an important job — she makes sure that everyone has sweet dreams rather than nightmares! But she needs her magic dream dust to do this. When her bag fell into the hands of the goblins, nobody in the human world or Fairyland could sleep peacefully!

**Without her dream dust, Sabrina has been known to sleep-fly!**

**Sabrina sometimes sings a beautiful lullaby that puts everyone to sleep!**

# Lisa
## the Lollipop Fairy

The Sugar & Spice Fairies keep sweet treats tasting delicious.

In Kirsty's hometown, the Candy Land candy factory is the place to visit. They make all kinds of delicious treats — and best of all, Kirsty's aunt Helen works there! But after Jack Frost stole the Sugar & Spice Fairies' magic charms, all candy tasted terrible. To defeat Jack Frost, the girls had to first track down Lisa the Lollipop Fairy's very special lollipop charm.

# Esme
## the Ice Cream Fairy

Jack Frost wanted to use the Sugar & Spice Fairies' charms to build himself a gigantic candy castle. Esme's ice cream charm was a part of his plan. But while he had her magic, ice cream everywhere was a melted mess. Rachel and Kirsty had to get Esme's charm back—and fast!

Esme's favorite ice cream flavor is mint chip.

# Coco
## the Cupcake Fairy

Wetherbury's Cupcake Corner was overrun by goblins in Coco's story. Jack Frost wanted lots of cupcakes to decorate his edible castle. Rachel, Kirsty, and Coco had to work together to take the bakery back!

# Clara
## the Chocolate Fairy

**T**he girls were finally going on a tour of Candy Land! They knew they had to track down Clara's cocoa bean charm, or the trip was sure to be a disaster. There were troublesome goblins everywhere masquerading as workers!

**Clara makes the best chocolate cake in Fairyland.**

# Madeline
## the Cookie Fairy

There was trouble afoot in the cookie wing of Candy Land. The cookies at the factory were coming out all wrong! Kirsty's aunt tried to solve the problem, but Rachel and Kirsty knew she was going to need some magic help.

**Madeline won the Fairyland Bake-Off competition three years in a row!**

# Layla
## the Cotton Candy Fairy

At the Wetherbury Park Fair, Rachel and Kirsty were on the lookout for Layla's charm. A sneaky goblin dressed as a clown seemed to have the only delicious cotton candy around — so they knew where to start. But the goblin wouldn't give up his charm easily — he was having too much fun!

# Nina
## the Birthday Cake Fairy

By the time Kirsty's birthday arrived, the girls only needed to find Nina's magic birthday cake charm. But this was an important one — Kirsty's birthday would be ruined without it!

Nina and Belle the Birthday Fairy make sure every fairy has a happy birthday.

# Hope
## the Happiness Fairy

The Princess Fairies are Fairyland royalty!

Rachel and Kirsty met the Princess Fairies when they were spending a week at the Golden Palace. It's a magical old castle where real princes and princesses once lived! The girls were whisked away to a Fairyland Ball by Polly the Party Fun Fairy. But Jack Frost crashed the ball and stole the royal fairies' tiaras! Without the tiaras, no human or fairy would ever have a magical time ever again!

The queen's magic sent the missing tiaras to the Golden Palace.

# Cassidy
## the Costume Fairy

The girls and their friends enjoyed exploring the Golden Palace in Cassidy's story — but they soon had to help Cassidy find her tiara so everyone could look beautiful at the Golden Palace pageant.

# Anya
## the Cuddly Creatures Fairy

The Golden Palace has its own petting zoo, and there are lots of different animals to meet there! But with Anya's golden tiara in the hands of the goblins, all the cuddly creatures are acting very strangely.

**Anya's magic keeps the special friendship between animals and humans strong.**

# Elisa
## the Royal Adventure Fairy

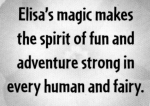

With Elisa's sparkly tiara missing, nobody wanted to have any fun! The girls had to track down the goblins to recover the tiara and return everyone's sense of adventure.

Elisa's magic makes the spirit of fun and adventure strong in every human and fairy.

Elisa likes to plan trips and treasure hunts for her fairy friends.

Each of the Princess Fairies' tiaras has a different-shaped jewel.

# Lizzie
## the Sweet Treats Fairy

It was time for a royal tea party at the Golden Palace and everyone was looking forward to eating lots of delicious things. But without Princess Lizzie's gold tiara to make sure everything tasted delicious, all of the sweet treats tasted terrible.

**Lizzie often swaps recipes with Cherry the Cake Fairy and Honey the Candy Fairy. Yummy!**

# Maddie
## the Fun and Games Fairy

Maddie the Fun and Games Fairy makes sure that kids everywhere enjoy games and playtime! But with her magic tiara missing, everyone at the Golden Palace was miserable. Rachel and Kirsty had to find the tiara before their field day was ruined!

**Maddie is riding a rocking horse when the girls discover her!**

The Princess Fairies

# Eva
## the Enchanted Ball Fairy

Rachel and Kirsty enjoy two wonderful balls — one at the Golden Palace and the other at the Fairyland Palace.

Eva's special magic makes sure that everyone is beautifully dressed for special parties and balls. But while Eva's tiara is gone, celebrations everywhere are a disaster. In this book, Rachel and Kirsty had to visit the scary Ice Castle to take Eva's tiara back from Jack Frost!

Jack Frost is such a troublemaker that the fairies have stopped inviting him to their parties!

# Jessie
## the Lyrics Fairy

The girls were so excited to return to Rainspell Island for a five-day music festival! But when they got there, they found out that Jack Frost had stolen the Superstar Fairies' magic clef necklaces. Without Jessie's necklace, none of the stars singing at pop music events anywhere could remember their words!

Jessie loves using her imagination to write song lyrics.

Jessie's pink boots were a present from Phoebe the Fashion Fairy.

# Adele
## the Voice Fairy

**A**dele's magic helps music stars in Fairyland and the human world sing on key! But with her magic necklace missing, no one could hit the right notes at the music festival. Well, aside from a mysterious new star named Gobby.

**In Adele's book, the girls get to meet their favorite boy band, A-OK!**

# Vanessa
## the Choreography Fairy

**B**eing able to dance is a very important part of being a superstar! Vanessa helps each star perfect their routines. In her story, it was almost time for music sensation Sasha Sharp to perform, but Sasha couldn't dance a single step!

**Vanessa's blue romper was handmade by Tyra the Designer Fairy.**

# Miley
## the Stylist Fairy

**M**iley's magic helps music stars look their very best. But at the Rainspell Music Festival, Miley's necklace went missing, and all the pop stars' clothes and accessories were in a terrible mess!

Miley is always on the lookout for the hottest new trend.

Jack Frost thinks he knows everything about fashion — take a peek at the Fashion Fairies books to find out more!

# Frankie
## the Makeup Fairy

**H**aving your face painted at a festival is always fun. But when Frankie's necklace went missing at the Rainspell event, all face paint and makeup looked horrible!

Frankie was in the same year at school as Miranda the Beauty Fairy.

# Alyssa
## the Star-spotter Fairy

**A**lyssa's skill is very special to all pop sensations — she spots new stars and makes sure that every one of them feels full of confidence. But with her magic clef in the hands of the goblins at the Rainspell festival, the search for new talent seemed to be over . . . until the girls saved the day!

# Cassie
## the Concert Fairy

Jack Frost's stage name is Jax Tempo.

Cassie's magic clef necklace makes sure concerts run smoothly, so when it went missing, the final concert of the Rainspell Music Festival went horribly wrong. The girls had to trick Jack Frost into returning the necklace so there could be a fabulous festival finale!

A magic music festival takes place in Fairyland at the same time as the Rainspell Music Festival!

Cassie loves pumpkin chocolate-chip cookies.

# Miranda
## the Beauty Fairy

The Fashion Fairies help fairies and humans look their best.

Miranda has over 100 lipsticks in her makeup collection!

When a brand-new shopping center opened in Tippington, Kirsty and Rachel decided to enter a charity fashion show where they could design their own clothes. But Jack Frost thought everyone in the world should dress like him, so he stole the seven Fashion Fairies' magic items — including Miranda's shimmery magic lipstick — to put his plan into action!

# Claudia
## the Accessories Fairy

It's great to have a pretty accessory to match an outfit! But with Claudia's magic necklace in the hands of Jack Frost and his goblins, accessories everywhere fell apart and lost all their sparkle.

Claudia always matches her headband to her shoes!

# Tyra
## the Designer Fairy

In Tyra's book, it was time for the girls to get creative at the design workshop! But with Tyra's magic tape measure missing, all the clothes in the Tippington Fountains Shopping Center were falling apart!

Tyra likes to design new dresses with Miley the Stylist Fairy!

# Alexa
## the Fashion
## Reporter Fairy

Jack Frost was determined to let everyone know about his crazy new fashion label, Ice Blue, and he used the magic of Alexa's stolen pen to do it! The girls had to track down the missing magic item before Jack Frost became the most famous fashion designer in the human world.

**Jack Frost interviews himself about his own fashion label!**

# Jennifer
## the Hairstylist
### Fairy

**W**hen your hair has been styled nicely, it makes you feel very special! But without Jennifer's special magic, everyone's hair looked very strange!

Jennifer loves to dye her hair bright red.

# Brooke
## the Photographer
### Fairy

**R**achel and Kirsty were taking part in a fashion photo shoot when Brooke appeared! Brooke's magic camera was missing, and when Jack Frost started acting like a model, the girls had a suspicion they knew where the camera might be . . .

# Lola
## the Fashion Show Fairy

I n this final Fashion Fairies' adventure, it was time for the Tippington Fountains fashion show! Kirsty and Rachel couldn't wait to be part of the fun and model their own designs on the catwalk. But Lola's magic backstage pass went missing, and the girls knew that without it, the fashion show would be a spectacular disaster!

Lola's sparkly silver boots are perfect for a night out dancing with Jade the Disco Fairy!

# Holly
## the Christmas Fairy

*Holly loves spreading Christmas cheer.*

Kirsty and Rachel met Holly on a trip to Fairyland just before Christmas. They discovered that Jack Frost had stolen Santa's sleigh! Without it, Santa couldn't deliver any presents to boys and girls in the human world. Holly needed the girls' help to find her three magic Christmas presents.

**Holly's scarlet dress was created for her by Santa's elves. It's made from the same material as Santa's suit!**

**Holly gives Santa's reindeer flying lessons every year!**

*Special Edition*

# Joy
## the Summer Vacation Fairy

Joy makes sure
summer vacation is
a special time!

**R**achel and Kirsty were excited to be returning to Rainspell Island for summer vacation! But things weren't how they remembered them at all . . . the sea was rough, the beach wasn't sandy, and even the ice cream tasted bad! The girls had to help Joy find her Rainspell shells and make summer vacation fun for everyone again!

When Joy uses her wand, lovely summery smells waft in the air!

Jack Frost stole the Rainspell shells because he didn't want anyone else to have a fun vacation.

# Stella
## the Star Fairy

Stella brings joy to the holiday season.

**E**ach year, Stella the Star Fairy uses her three magic Christmas tree decorations to make sure that everyone's Christmas is happy and fun. But when Jack Frost stole the magic decorations, the special time of year looked like it might end up dark and miserable for everyone.

**Stella and Holly the Christmas Fairy are best friends!**

**Stella and Holly help all the other fairies decorate their homes!**

# Kylie
## the Carnival Fairy

Sunnydays Carnival comes to town only once a year. Everyone usually has a great time going on the rides, playing games, and watching the parades. But the year Rachel and Kirsty met Kylie, Jack Frost and his goblins were at the carnival, too! They stole Kylie's three magic hats and everything started to go wrong.

**Kylie's outfit showcases all the joy and fun of the carnival! Her skirt twirls in a rainbow of color and the ribbons in her hair dance in the breeze.**

# Paige
## the Christmas Play Fairy

Paige knows that the Christmas show must go on!

W hen they met Paige, Kirsty and Rachel were going to act in *Cinderella*. But things were not going well. Paige's three magic shoes were missing, so the costumes didn't fit, the scenery was breaking, and nobody could remember their lines!

Paige's favorite ballet is *Sleeping Beauty*!

# Flora
## the
## Dress-Up Fairy

In this magical story, Kirsty and Rachel stayed in a real castle! Kirsty's cousin, Lindsay, had planned a wonderful costume ball. The girls couldn't wait to get dressed up! But when they stumbled across Jack Frost at the castle, they knew Lindsay's ball was in trouble. Flora needed their help to protect her three magic items from the goblins!

Flora's favorite spell is one that turns old clothes into perfect party outfits!

Flora's magic items are a figurine, a cape, and a mask. They make sure that all parties go without a hitch.

The crown of shells worn by Flora was made for her by Shannon the Ocean Fairy.

# Addison
## the April Fool's Day Fairy

Addison helps to keep a silly spirit alive on April 1st.

J okes were falling flat when Addison's magic items went missing. Rachel and Kirsty had only a day to return everyone's sense of humor. Luckily, the goblins didn't stand a chance against the girls!

Addison loves making up her own knock-knock jokes.

Addison and Juliet the Valentine Fairy share the same birthday.

Shannon keeps watch over all the oceans.

The girls were visiting Kirsty's grandma in the seaside town of Leamouth when they were magically invited to a Fairyland beach party! Here they met Shannon — who told them that Jack Frost had stolen her three enchanted pearls!

Shannon makes two bubbles to go over Rachel's and Kirsty's heads that let them breathe and speak underwater!

Lucky Shannon is friends with all of the ocean creatures and the Ocean Fairies!

# Gabriella
## the Snow Kingdom Fairy

**Gabriella helps keep winter fun and festive!**

Rachel and Kirsty were having a wonderful snowy vacation in the mountains when they met Gabriella! They were really looking forward to skiing, snowboarding, and going to the Winter Festival. But no such luck — everything seemed to be going wrong! Gabriella needed Rachel and Kirsty's help to find her magic snowflake, chest full of festive spirit, and firestone so she could put things right.

**Gabriella and Crystal the Snow Fairy are best friends!**

**The Winter Olympics happen every four years. Gabriella is always there!**

# Mia
## the Bridesmaid Fairy

Mia's magic protects weddings.

Rachel and Kirsty were counting down the days until they were bridesmaids for Kirsty's cousin Esther! Preparations were going very well, but a visit from Mia the Bridesmaid Fairy changed everything — something was wrong with her three magic wedding charms. The girls had to help Mia so that Esther's wedding wasn't a total disaster!

Mia's wedding charms are a shiny penny, golden bells, and a silver veil!

# Destiny
## the Rock Star Fairy

Destiny keeps music stars shining brightly.

Destiny works closely with the seven Superstar Fairies to look after all rock music!

Rachel and Kirsty's favorite girl group is The Angels!

Destiny's three magic objects are the sparkly sash, which perfects music stars' outfits; the keepsake key, which looks after all songs and music; and the magic microphone, which makes sound and lighting work! But Jack Frost took these magic items from Destiny because he wanted to be the best music star in town.

# Belle
## the Birthday Fairy

In Belle's story, Rachel and her dad had planned a surprise birthday party for Rachel's mom. But nothing seemed to be going right and the two girls knew something was wrong in Fairyland . . . they needed to help Belle make birthdays fantastic once again!

Belle and the Party Fairies are always working together to make every fairy's special day magical.

Jack Frost hates birthdays because he doesn't want anyone to know how old he is!

102

# Juliet
## the Valentine Fairy

**W**ho doesn't like Valentine's Day? Jack Frost, that's who! He tried to ruin it one year by stealing Juliet's magic objects. With these objects in the hands of the goblins — plus a wand to cause extra trouble — the magic of Valentine's Day looked sure to be destroyed!

Juliet's magic objects are a Valentine's card, a red rose, and a box of candy hearts.

# Trixie
## the Halloween Fairy

Trick or treat!
Trixie's magic
makes Halloween
spooky and fun.

Rachel and Kirsty couldn't wait to go trick-or-treating in Tippington! Every year, the children dress up and have a really great time. But a visit from Trixie the Halloween Fairy put the girls on high alert — the greedy goblins had stolen her three Halloween treats and with them missing, nobody could have any Halloween fun.

**With Trixie, the girls meet a little black kitten named Moonlight.**

# Cheryl
## the Christmas Tree Fairy

Cheryl's magic helps make Christmas really special.

Decorating a Christmas tree is an important part of Christmas. In this book Rachel and Kirsty discovered that Cheryl's Fairyland Christmas tree was missing. This special tree helps keep the season magical. Without it, the Christmas celebrations couldn't begin!

Jack Frost has taken Cheryl's magic objects because he wants his Christmas to be the only one that's any fun!

Cheryl also has a magic Christmas star and Christmas gift.

# Florence
## the Friendship Fairy

Florence watches over best friends — like Rachel and Kirsty.

Everyone knows just how important friendship is, so Florence really is a very special fairy! Her three magic objects look after all aspects of friendship — her memory book keeps happy memories safe, her friendship ribbon lets friends have lots of fun together, and her sparkly bracelet helps friends get along. But when Florence lost her objects, Kirsty and Rachel had to use their special friendship to save the day.

Every year, Florence organizes a special Friendship Day to celebrate friendships everywhere!

In this story Florence and the other fairies make Rachel and Kirsty special friendship bracelets, to say thank you for being such great friends!

# Emma
## the Easter Fairy

Emma and her magic eggs keep Easter safe.

Emma's pet chicken, Fluffy, lays three magic eggs every year!

A visit from Emma meant Rachel and Kirsty's holiday needed help. The Easter bunny had gone missing and Emma's three magic eggs had been stolen! The girls had to help out before Easter was ruined.

# Autumn
## the Falling Leaves Fairy

Jack Frost loves ice and snow. He thought that he could take Autumn's magic objects, skip fall, and go right to winter. But that's not how nature works! Rachel and Kirsty had to act fast to keep the seasons on track.

**Autumn loves to knit.**

# Selena
## the Sleepover Fairy

**W**hen Rachel and Kirsty went to a big sleepover at a museum, strange things started to happen. The girls suspected it had something to do with a group of children with green skin and very big noses. The best friends helped Selena as much as they could.

Selena's three magic objects are a sleeping bag, a games bag, and a snacks box.

Selena often hangs out with Sabrina the Sweet Dreams Fairy.

# Natalie
## the Christmas Stocking Fairy

Natalie's magic makes sure opening presents on Christmas morning is a time full of joy and happiness.

**Natalie's wand sends out glittery silver snowflakes whenever she casts a spell.**

Without her magic stocking, pie, and candy cane, Natalie worried Christmas morning wouldn't be magical at all!

# Keira
## the Movie Star Fairy

Keira's magic looks after all movie stars.

**R**achel and Kirsty met Keira when they were extras in a real Hollywood movie being filmed in Tippington! Things started to go wrong on set, and the girls soon received a visit from this very glamorous fairy. Keira needed help finding her silver script, magic megaphone, and enchanted clapboard.

FILM SCRIPT

Tyra the Designer Fairy made Keira's long red silk dress.

Alyssa the Star-spotter Fairy was the one who spotted Keira's flair for film!

# Olympia
## the Games Fairy

Olympia makes sure sports competitions run smoothly.

**O**lympia is the most athletic fairy in Fairyland! She uses her magic to make sure that sports, games, and tournaments in the human world and Fairyland are fun, organized and — above all — fair!

Olympia's magic objects are a sparkling swimming cap, a musical bicycle bell, and a pair of sneakers.

Olympia's magic watches over the Melford Triathlon, the Fairyland Games, and the Fairyland Olympics!

# Brianna
## the Tooth Fairy

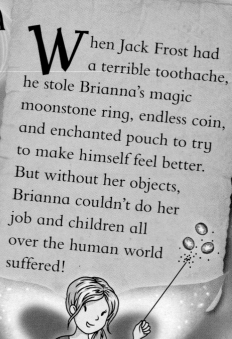

**W**hen Jack Frost had a terrible toothache, he stole Brianna's magic moonstone ring, endless coin, and enchanted pouch to try to make himself feel better. But without her objects, Brianna couldn't do her job and children all over the human world suffered!

Brianna collects lost teeth from children all over the world!

Zara the Starlight Fairy sometimes lights Brianna's way to lost teeth.

Brianna loves chatting to nighttime creatures!

# Cara
## the Camp Fairy

Cara's magic keeps camp extra fun for everyone.

Cara the Camp Fairy loves camping in the great outdoors. But Jack Frost doesn't understand the appeal. He thought that no one should enjoy going to camp, so he took Cara's magic items. Fortunately, Rachel and Kirsty were spending the week at Camp Oakwood. Once they were on the case, Jack Frost's goblins didn't stand a chance!

Cara's favorite camp activities are hiking and archery.

Rachel and Kirsty's group at camp is called the Rocky Raccoons.

# Read them all!

## The Rainbow Fairies

## The Weather Fairies

## The Party Fairies

## The Jewel Fairies

## The Pet Fairies

## The Fun Day Fairies

# The
# Petal Fairies

# The
# Dance Fairies

# The
# Sports Fairies

# The
# Music Fairies

# The Magical
# Animal Fairies

# The
# Earth Fairies

# The
## Ocean Fairies

# The
## Night Fairies

# The Sugar & Spice
## Fairies

# The
## Princess Fairies

# The
## Superstar Fairies

# The
## Fashion Fairies

# Special Editions